Dedication and Acknowledgments

It was a joy to revisit the characters from my play *Have You Filled a Bucket Today?* while writing this book. I sincerely hope that BFF, Trey, and Mimi inspire children to be bucket fillers.

First, I'd like to thank author Carol McCloud without whose support the play and this book would not be possible.

To the teachers, librarians, principals, and littlest readers who have supported me all along: Thank you. May you always remember that, "The more you read the more things you know. The more that you learn the more places you'll go." -Dr. Seuss

Meghan Reynolds: Thank you for your guidance and editing prowess (and reigning me in when necessary!).

Shawn Forster and Lisa Hix McGork: You have been with me throughout this entire process. I am grateful for your insights and blessed by your friendship and laughter.

Tiffany Zook, my business manager extraordinaire: Thank you for your enthusiasm, wisdom, and friendship.

My nieces and nephews, Catie, Lizzy, Lexie, Maddie, Jasper, James, and Charlotte: May you always be bucket fillers and may others fill your buckets, too.

I send much love and appreciation to: My angel of a mom, my first and best teacher, and my accountant dad, my trusted advisor. I am a writer in part because you taught me that I could be anything I wanted to be. And to my siblings, the inspiration behind the Strawberry Hill setting. Kim: you're the best sister and friend and Aunt Bim anyone could ask for. Kurt: you're the perfect mix of annoying little brother, great friend, and Uncle Doo. I'm grateful to have you all in my life.

I would like to dedicate this book to my three boys. To my sons, Trey and Trevor: Your silliness, your sweetness, and your "drama" live in these characters. Thank you for filling my bucket every day. And last but not least, to my husband, Gregg: Thank you for believing in me and for supporting this—and every—dream.

-A.M.G.H.

www.mascotbooks.com

Bucket Filling Fairy

For more information, please contact:
Mascot Books
560 Herndon Parkway #120
Herndon, VA 20170
info@mascotbooks.com

Library of Congress Control Number: 2015914688

CPSIA Code: PRT1015A
ISBN-13: 978-1-63177-175-0

Printed in the United States

Bucket Filling Fairy

Written by

Ann Marie Gardinier Halstead

Illustrated by **Sydni Kruger**

To the wonderful students at St. Aloysius Catholic School— Happy Bucket Filling! :) AMG Halstead

It was an ordinary day at Strawberry Hill Summer Camp…that is, until Trey pushed Jasper into the art table and paint splashed everywhere! Their counselor, Mimi, was so upset, her face turned as red as the strawberry on her shirt. Before Mimi could say a word, a visitor magically appeared.

"Hi, friends! I know you're surprised by the look on your face;
so now that I'm here, I will state my case.
Bucket Filling Fairy is my name
and bucket filling is my game.

Gee oh gee, boy oh boy,
filling buckets brings so much joy!
My friends call me BFF and you can too.
There's so much I want to share with you!"

All of the campers were excited—all except for Trey.

"Your timing is perfect, BFF. I was just about to talk to Trey and the other campers about bucket filling," said Mimi.

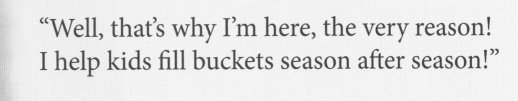

"Well, that's why I'm here, the very reason!
I help kids fill buckets season after season!"

Trey rolled his eyes. He already knew about
bucket filling; he learned about it at school.
He didn't want to hear about it again,
especially from a rhyming fairy.

Mimi reminded Trey that he hadn't filled many buckets since he'd been at camp. In fact, he'd dipped a lot of buckets.

"I've heard about you, young friend; it's why I'm here.
I want to help, to show that I care.
I can help you see that buckets are for filling,
and making people happy can be so thrilling!"

Spitting confetti out of his mouth, Trey said, "I don't
see what the big deal is. It's not like I'm the meanest
kid at camp or something."

"No one said that, Trey,"
Mimi replied, kindly.
"But is it possible you've
done some things that
were hurtful to others?"

"Well, no one said I hurt
their feelings."

Mimi explained, "Remember, Trey; you fill someone's bucket when you say or do kind things. You dip someone's bucket when you say or do unkind things. Your friends may not tell you when you've dipped their buckets, but I have a feeling you know when you do."

"Well, if everyone thinks
I'm such a bucket dipper,
why doesn't Bucket Filling
Fairy just change me into
a bucket filler? You're
magical, aren't you?"

"I'd never call you a dipper,
Trey; that would be a curse.
Labels like that
are just the worst!
Now I will use my magic
to help you to see,
but how you treat others,
well, that's not up to me."

Before Trey realized what
was happening, BFF
sprinkled him with fairy
dust and said,

"Drama mama,
    spaghetti confetti,
    fireflies
        to open Trey's eyes!"

In a flash Trey
began to really
see the things he'd
done to the other
kids at camp…

…he pointed and laughed at Charlotte's
costume during the costume party.

…he ignored the new kid, James, who tried to talk to him.

…he excluded Maddie and Jasper
from the basketball game during free time.

…he tripped his
little brother Trevor
during soccer. His
own brother!

Trey looked at Mimi and BFF and said, "I guess you're right. I have been dipping buckets and hurting people's feelings."

"Oh Trey,
I'm glad that you're learning,

but all that dipping
makes my stomach start churning!"

Trey felt sick too, thinking he was the
one who made the other kids upset.
Even his own brother!

Mimi asked, "Trey, do you know why you've been acting this way? Do you have any idea why kids dip buckets?"

He thought about it and said, "I don't know. Maybe they think they're being funny. But I guess they're not. Or maybe their buckets are empty and they think they can fill them by dipping other kids' buckets."

"And does that work?" Mimi asked.

"No. The best way to fill your bucket
is to fill someone else's bucket, right?"

"Exactly. Good for you, Trey!"

But Trey looked worried. "I really messed up," he said. "What if the other kids don't want to be friends with me after the way I treated them?"

Then Trey smiled as he remembered something. "My mom says that everyone makes mistakes. What's important is that we apologize and make better choices the next time."

"Your mama is smart. She's exactly right.
Filling keeps us happy both day and night!"

Trey took his mom's advice that very minute! He apologized to the other kids and asked for the chance to be a better friend.

The other campers seemed surprised, but they accepted Trey's apology. As he walked back toward Mimi and BFF, he thought about how full his bucket was and how lucky he was to have such forgiving friends.

"Mimi! BFF! They accepted my apology!" Trey exclaimed.

"Oh, Trey, you've come so far.
I think you're becoming a bucket filling star."

"I don't know about that," Trey said, blushing.

"Well,
I certainly do.
You're growing and changing;
that much is true.
You've learned that my magic
is fun and it's pure,
but you've learned that my magic
isn't your cure.

To change yourself,
your heart must be your guide;
only you can change
who you are inside.

Now there's one more thing
that I'd like you to do;
we'll call it
your Bucket Filling Lesson:
Part Two."

Mimi and BFF asked Trey to help teach the other campers about bucket filling. Trey wasn't sure he was the best kid for the job, but Mimi reminded him that he'd filled his friends' buckets by apologizing.

"You can do this; have no fear.
But first, there's something that you have to wear.
Mimi, I think it's time to recognize Trey,
for learning about the bucket filling way.
For becoming a Super Bucket Filler, you deserve a prize.
I have a feeling it's just the right size."

"Wow! Thanks, BFF. This is awesome,"
Trey said, running around like a superhero.

"Trey, why don't you rehearse what you'd like to say to the other campers," Mimi suggested.

"Now you know I love magic and I think it's about time, so I'll help you to speak your lesson in rhyme.

Drama mama, spaghetti confetti, lemons and limes, help Trey with rhymes!"

Trey began slowly and hesitantly.

"I've learned so much from our time here today.
When dealing with others there is only one way.
Be kind to each and every person you meet;
help them, include them, offer them a seat.
Filling buckets is the very best thing you can do.
It makes others feel good and makes you feel good too!"

BUCKET FILLING POEM

"Oh, Trey, teaming up with you
has been such a pleasure.
Bucket fillers like you
are truly a treasure!
Now it's time to bring our sweet message home.
Join me in reciting the Bucket Filling Poem!"

"When I fill someone's bucket, I make them feel great.

We all know that love is much better than hate.

When I fill someone's bucket, I fill mine up too.

It makes me feel happy when I am blue.

So be kind, help others, show your appreciation.

Before you know it, we'll be a bucket filling nation!"

"Spending time with you both has been so much fun.
But it's clear to me that my work here is done.
It's been a delight to meet you. So long for now.
I'll say goodbye with a wave and a bow."

Photo Credit: Robert Young

About the Author

Ann Marie Gardinier Halstead is a professor, writer, speaker, and bullying-prevention advocate. She is the author of the bullying-prevention play *Have You Filled a Bucket Today?* (starring Bucket Filling Fairy!) based on the award-winning books by Carol McCloud. Ann Marie has discussed bullying-prevention programming on the radio (*NCPR, Parenting Matters Radio, Dr. On Call, Motherhood with Dr. Christina Hibbert*) and television (*Talented People, The Big Picture With Thom Hartmann*). In addition to writing plays and children's books, she blogs for *The Huffington Post, 30 Second Mom,* and *Team Bossy Gals,* and has also been published in *edutopia, Compact Impact,* and *Southern Theatre.* Her bullying-prevention song, "The Bucket Filling Song," is available on iTunes. Ann Marie lives in Richmond, Virginia with her husband, two sons, and a 90 pound German Shepard.

For More Information

To order a copy of *Have You Filled a Bucket Today?* or to learn more about producing the play at your school or theatre, please visit www.bucketfillingplay.com.

If you liked "The Bucket Filling Poem" in the book, download "The Bucket Filling Song" at www.itunes.com, lyrics by the author and music by Peaceful Schools. Search by title or artist (Peaceful Schools).

To contact the author about visiting your school, please email her at info@bucketfillingplay.com.